¡Qué quilombo, che!

Néstor Barron

¡Qué quilombo, che!

Barron's guide
Beware of the chanta

Ediciones Continente

¡Qué quilombo, che!

Diseño de tapa: Omar Tavalla
Diseño de interior: Carlos Almar

Barron, Néstor
  ¡Qué quilombo, che! : beware of the chanta, barron's guide . - 1a ed. -
Ciudad Autónoma de Buenos Aires : Continente, 2014.
  96 p. ; 20x14 cm.

  ISBN 978-950-754-492-7

  1. Diccionarios.
  CDD 030

© **Ediciones Continente**
Pavón 2229 (C1248AAE) Buenos Aires, Argentina
Tel.: (5411) 4308-3535 - Fax: (5411) 4308-4800
www.edicontinente.com.ar
e-mail: info@edicontinente.com.ar

Queda hecho el depósito que marca la ley 11.723.

Se imprimieron 3.000 ejemplares.

Libro de edición argentina

No se permite la reproducción parcial o total, el almacenamiento, el alquiler, la transmisión o la transformación de este libro, en cualquier forma o por cualquier medio, sea electrónico o mecánico, mediante fotocopias, digitalización u otros métodos, sin el permiso previo y escrito del editor. Su infracción está penada por las leyes 11.723 y 25.446.

Este libro se terminó de imprimir en el mes de diciembre de 2014,
en **Cooperativa Chilavert Artes Gráficas**,
Chilavert 1136, CABA, Argentina – (5411) 4924-7676 – imprentachilavert@gmail.com
(Empresa recuperada y autogestionada por sus trabajadores)

Las tapas fueron impresas en **Cooperativa de Trabajo Obrera Gráfica Campichuelo Limitada**,
Campichuelo 553, CABA, Argentina – (5411) 4981-6500 – presupuestos@cogcal.com.ar
(Empresa autogestionada por sus trabajadores)

Encuadernado en **Cooperativa de Trabajo La Nueva Unión Ltda.**,
Patagones 2746, CABA, Argentina – (5411) 4911-1586 – cooplanuevaunion@yahoo.com.ar
(Empresa recuperada y autogestionada por sus trabajadores)

Las tapas fueron laminadas en **Cooperatia Gráfica 22 de Mayo (ex Lacabril)**,
Av. Bernardino Rivadavia 700, Avellaneda, Bs. As., Argentina
– (5411) 4208-1150 – lanuevalacabril@gmail.com
(Empresa recuperada y autogestionada por sus trabajadores)

INDEX

Presentación / Introduction 7

Part 1
The Buenos Aires Slang
Words & Colloquial Expressions 11

Part 2
A Brief English-Argentinian Guide 85

PRESENTACIÓN

Toda cultura tiene su subcultura, pero en general no es algo que se aprenda en los libros de gramática. El autor de esta guía absorbió varios idiomas de la gente en las calles de otras ciudades, eso gracias a la hospitalidad que encontró. Como resultado de la experiencia era inevitable que desarrollara un listado para los forasteros que caminan las calles de Buenos Aires. El castellano que hablan los argentinos es diferente a todos los demás. Hay frases que se construyen de otra forma, los verbos se conjugan con variantes, y las palabras que usamos también cambian: poco tiene parecido con el castellano que se ha aprendido en las clases de idioma.

Ningún diccionario puede ser total, simplemente porque un idioma es un ejercicio en movimiento. Y los lenguajes de las subculturas se mueven con velocidad mayor aun. Nótese que la tradición, historia y lírica del tango tienen un léxico propio, en partes aun en uso (ej. *canyengue*, algo desvencijado, de baja factura, se usa con frecuencia), con bibliografía abundante, algo de ella trasladada a la música moderna, como en las referencias a las drogas (ej. *paco*, la pasta base más dañina). Y hay otra subclase, la jerga que se le atribuye a la población carcelaria y criminal donde originó el habla al revés, *alvesre* (ej. *chabomba*, para bombacha), antiguo ya, con códigos e identidad diferentes pero en uso todavía en el habla diaria. Mucho de todo eso no se puede incluir en este volumen, cuya intención es ser de rápida consulta. Pero los que sienten curiosidad por la lingüística local hallarán numerosas fuentes de referencia en otros textos.

Andrew Graham-Yooll

INTRODUCTION

Every culture has its subculture, but it isn't something learned from grammar books. The author of this book has learned several languages from the people in the streets of other cities — this was thanks to their fine hospitality. As a result it seemed inevitable that something should be compiled for foreigners who walk the streets of Buenos Aires. The Spanish language that Argentine (or Argentinian, if preferred) people speak is different to any other. Phrases are constructed differently, so are verbal conjugations, and the words that we use daily also change: nothing is similar to whatever you have learned in your Spanish language classes.

No dictionary is complete, simply because language is a moving object. And the languages of subcultures are an even faster moving object. Hence note that tango tradition, history and lyrics, has a whole lexicon of its own, some still in use (e.g. *canyengue*, which means dilapidated, of low class, which is often used), with an abundant bibliography, and some that has been moved into modern music, as in references to drugs (e.g. *paco*, which is a low grade extremely harmful form of cocaine). And we have another subclass, the jargon of the criminal world and prisons, where *alvesre*, i.e. turned round, see *chabomba*, for example, began and became a code with its own identity. Much of that, of course, had to be held out of this volume, intended as a handy, rapid result, reference. But for those curious about local linguistics the broader references are elsewhere.

Andrew Graham-Yooll

YOUR ATTENTION PLEASE...

1) Spanish pronunciation turns on *the vowels*. There's *only one way* to pronounce each one; if you get it right, you will be in touch with Spanish native speakers everywhere. Take note: **A** as in Apple. **E** as in Egg. **I** as in It. **O** as in Orange. **U** as in Uma (Thurman, the actress).

2) There are words indicated with **(adj)**, for *adjective*. Except when expressly indicated, adjectives appear only in the masculine form, which end in "**o**", and in a few cases in "**e**". For the feminine form, change "o" or "e" for "**a**". For example: Buen*o* – Buen*a,* Lind*o* – Lind*a,* Bolud*o* – Bolud*a,* Divertid*o* – Divertid*a,* Amarret*e* – Amarret*a,* Alcahuet*e* – Alcahuet*a*

3) Verbs –indicated with **(v)** - are all in infinitive, finishing in *ar*, *er* or *ir*.

We speak a language of our own, *lunfardo* (Buenos Aires slang), heavily influenced by immigration and tango. This book will help engage in the new tongue. By the way: we talk too much. We can't stop. Chatting is a kind of national sport. So it's best to know some of the slang: to better enjoy street life in this crazy, melancholic and iconoclastic city called Good Airs.

There's one underlying warning in understanding this city: beware of the *chanta*.

Remember: this is not a technical book. It is intended for the reader in the company of an Argentine friend who happens to be explaining life around them. You are promised one thing: with this book, you will talk *lunfardo* just about as well as we Argentines speak the English language: it's not a lot, but more than nothing.

Néstor Barron
www.nestorbarron.com.ar

Part 1

The Buenos Aires Slang
Words & Colloquial Expressions

Abollado (adj)
1. Half crazy.
2. Stunned, light-headed, giddy.
(lit.) Dented.

Abrochar (v)
To cheat successfully someone.
(lit.) To button up.

Aceitar (v)
To bribe someone.
(lit.) To put oil in.

Afanar (v)
1. To steal.
2. Over charging for a service or a sale.
3. To win a game or something similar by a large score.

Afano
1. Theft, steal.

2. "*Ganamos por afano*": we win by a great difference in the score (it's used not only about games and matchs, but methaphorically too).

Aguantar (v)

1. To wait for.
2. To support and/or physically stand by someone. "Fuimos a aguantar a Boca" = 'We went to cheer Boca" (Note: Boca it's the most popular soccer team from Argentine).
3. To loan money or an object as a friendly act of support. "Si no tenés para la entrada te aguanto unos mangos" = "If you don't have money for the ticket I can lend you some".
4. To remain in a place or state for someone else's benefit.
(lit.) To endure.

Alcahuete (adj)

1. One who gives reports to the police, an informer.
2. Someone to whom you cannot entrust a secret.
3. Traitor.
See also: Batidor, Batilana.

Alcahuetear (v)

1. To give a report to the police.
2. To give away a secret, to tattle about a personal confidence.
3. To betray a secret from a friend.

Amarrete (adj)

A greedy one, a cheapskate, a haggler,

Amarrocar (v)

To raise money or possessions in an avaricious way.

Año Verde

An imaginary time where extraordinary things will happen. For exemple: "Argentine Año Verde" supposes that the country is led by honest politicians and there is no corruption, that the public services work fine, etc.

(lit.) The green year.

Aparato (adj)

(Same for both genres)
1. Silly person.
2. Lamer, dork, dumbass.
3. An asshole.
4. An eccentric person, in a bad sense.

(lit.) Apparatus.

Apolillar (v)

1. To sleep (in a general sense).
2. To sleep deeply and with carelessness.

Atorranta (adj/f)

Referred to a woman: lustful, even prostitute.

Atorrante (adj/m)

Referred to a man:
1. Lazy, unworried and sloppy person.
2. Sometimes, this word is used to refer to someone of reproachable, even punishable habits.
3. In other cases it can be used in a good sense, and it means "a nice guy, a charming fellow".

Ave Negra

A lawyer.

(lit.) A black bird, like the raven.

Autobombo

Self-advertising. From *auto* = *self*, and *bombo* = a bass drum used in political meetings and strikes, presumably to call for attention.

Babosear (v)

To make sexual and lust insinuations to another person.
(lit.) Slobbering

Baboso (adj)

Lustful and in some way pathetic person, who cannot control his/her sexual desires and makes inappropiate insinuations in the wrong time and the wrong place.
(lit.) Slobbering person.

Bacán (adj)

Rich person, who enjoy the life in great style. Like the French "Bon vivant".
(Femenine: Bacana)

Bagarto (adj)

(Same for both genres, but specially for women)
Ugly and grotesque person.

Bagayo (adj)

(Same for both genres, but specially for women)
1. Ugly person. It's a really disparaging word.
2. Luggage.

Bajón

"Have a *bajón*" means to be in a very melancholic mood.

Banana (adj)

(Same for both genres)
1. Referred to someone, it means *cool*, but in a sarcastic sense.
2. One of the words for penis.

Bancar (v)

1. To support a friend, to help him in many ways.
2. Otherwise, the word means to tolerate somebody that bores us or upsets us.
3. To finance (something or somebody).

Baqueteado (adj)

It refers both to objects and, metaphorically, to persons. It means very worn-out, too much used up.

Baquetear (v)

To use excessively an object, until leave it almost useless.

Baranda

A very bad smell.

Bárbaro (adj)

1. Great, wonderful, excellent, very well done, terrific, marvellous. (This adjective is used constantly, with these and many other similar meanings.)
2. Okay.
3. "¡Qué bárbaro!" means something like "Oh boy !".

Bardear (v)

To turn a normal circunstance in a chaos... sometimes a fun one.

Bardo

1. Chaos (in a general sense).
2. A crazy situation.
3. A complicated situation.

Barullo

Annoying noise.

Basurear (v)

To treat someone badly.

(lit.) From "Basura" = Garbage, in the sense of "To make garbage with someone".

See also: Forrear.

Batidor (adj)

One who gives reports to the police, an informer.

See also: Alcahuete, Batilana.

Batilana (adj)

(Same for both genres)
One who gives reports to the police, an informer.

See also: Alcahuete, Batidor.

Berreta (adj)

(Same for both genres)
Cheap, cheesy.

Berretín

A caprice, a silly illusion.

Bestia

One who is wonderful in something. "I really like Madonna, she's a bestia".

(lit.) Beast.

Bicho (adj)

(Same for both genres)
1. Ugly person.
2. Bad person.

(lit.) Insect

See also: Mal bicho

Bicicleta

Commercial deception.

Bife

1. Beefsteak.
2. Slap in face.

Biorsi

Bathroom.

Birra

Beer, brew.

(lit.) from the Italian word for.

Bizarro (adj)

Weird (referred to something or somebody).

Blanca

Cocaine

(lit.) White.

Bocha

1. A lot.
2. Indicates a great quantity of something. Exemple: "She had *bocha de libros* (a lot of books)".

Bocho

1. Head
2. As an adjetive, it means someone very smart and clever (Same for both genres).
3. "Hacerse el bocho" ("Make yourself the head") = To think too much about some matter.

Bola / Bolas

1. One of the words for *testicles*.
2. Rumour.
3. It's also used in many senses, according at the moment or situation. A few exemples:
—In the sense of *pay attention*: "Dame bola" ("Give me ball") = Pay attention to me; "Nadie le da bola" ("Nobody gives ball to him") = Nobody pay attention to him.
—In the sense of *annoying*: "Me rompe las bolas" ("She breaks my balls") = She really upsets me.
—In the sense of *boring*: "Tu amigo me hincha las bolas" ("Your friend fills my balls"") = Your friend really boring me.
—In the sense of *something that lacks*: "Estoy en bolas" ("I'm in my balls") = I don't have anything, *or* I don't know anything about this subject, *or* I'm haven't nothing to protect me.
—In the sense of *nudity*: "Estoy en bolas" ("I'm in my balls") = I'm naked.

(lit.) Ball, Balls
See also: Pelota / Pelotas.

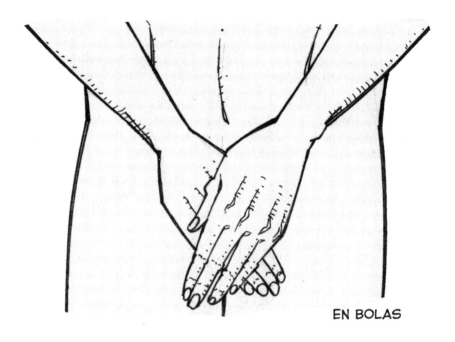

EN BOLAS

Bolazo

Big lie, exaggeration, bullshit, something impossible or incredible.
(lit.) Big ball.

Boleado (adj)

Stonned, confused.

Boleta (adj)

(Same for both genres)
Used in the sense of an adjective for "killed" in expressions like "You're *boleta*" for "You're dead, man", or "They did make him the *boleta*" for "They killed him".

(lit.) Invoice, receipt, voucher of payment.

Boleto

Lie.
(lit.) Bus ticket.

Boliche

Dance club.

Bolita

Contemptuous word for "Bolivian people".
(lit.) Little ball.

Bolonqui

A disorder, a chaotic and untidy situation.
See also: Quilombo.

Boludez

1. Thing that doesn't matter.
2. Stupid idea.

See also: Pelotudez.

Boludo (adj)

It's used in many senses, according at the moment or situation. A few exemples:
—*Fool, silly, asshole*: "Sos un boludo" ("You're an asshole")
—It's also a friendly form between friends, used in whatever situation: as a salutation, as a friendly adjective in the sense of "buddy", "man" or "my friend", even as an admirative exclamation like "Oh boy" or "Wow" ("¡Boludo, no te puedo creer!" = "Wow, it's amazing!"). In all those friendly senses it's used all the time, permanently, almost in every phrase.
—"Hacerse el boludo" (Play the fool) means "To pretend misunderstand" for to take advantage of a situation: "Se hace el boludo" (He plays the fool).

(lit.) One with big testicles.
See also: Pelotudo.

Bombacha
Women panties.

Bombero
Lesbian.
(lit.) Fireman.

Bombo
1. Womb of the pregnant women. "She have the bombo" means "She's pregned".
2. "Hacer bombo" ("Make the drum"): To make excessive and tendentious encomium about someone.

(lit.) Bass drumm

Bombón (adj)
(Same for both genres)
A very sexy and attractive person.

(lit.) Chocolate candy

Bondi
Public bus, also called "Colectivo", which means Collective transport.

Bonete
Used in the sense of *loosing mind* in phrases like "Está *del bonete*" ("He's *by his cap*", which means "He's crazy").

(lit.) Biretta or College cap

See also: Coco, Gorra, Peluca, Tomate.

Borrego
A boy, a kid.
(lit.) Lamb's puppy.

Bosta (adj)
(Same for both genres)
Used for persons or things: very bad.
(lit.) Shit (of horses or cows)

Bostero (adj)
Fan of the Buenos Aires-based and world wide famous football club Boca Juniors. Actually it refers to the really bad smell of the Riachuelo, a little river nearby the Boca stadium.
(lit.) From "bosta" = cattle excrement. "Bostero" = "One that smell like cattle excrement".

Botón
1. A cup, a policeman.
2. One who gives reports to the police, an informer.
(lit.) Button
See also: Alcahuete, Batidor, Buchón.

Brasuca
Contemptuous word for "Brasilian people".

Brutal (adj)
Marvelous, awesome
(lit.) Brutal, beastly.

Buchón (adj)
One who gives reports to the police, an informer.

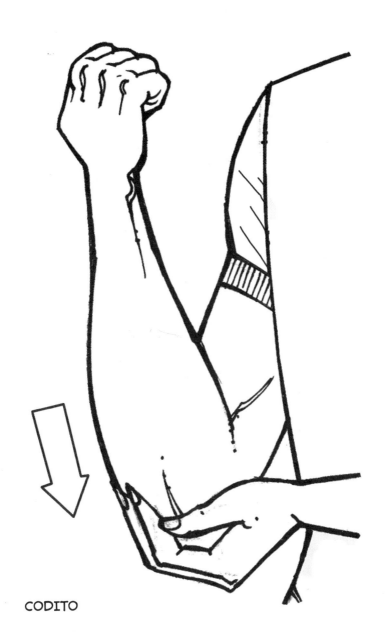

(lit.) Big mouth.
See also: Alcahuete, Batidor, Botón.
(Femenine: Buchona)

Bulín

A place used by engaged people to have sex with occasional partners.

Bulto

Penis and testicles that seems a package under the pants.

(lit.) package
See also: Paquete.

Buraco

1. A hole, an orifice.
2. A hole made by a bullet, a perforating wound.

Busarda

Fat abdomen.

Cábala

Gestures, habits or repetitive actions that someone practises always in order that it gives him good luck.

Caber (v)

To like something or someone, could be a friend, a sport, a hobby, a drink, a job, a place, anything. "El jazz me cabe" = I really like jazz music.

(lit.) To fit into.

Cabulero (adj)

Person who has any *cábala* (see)

Cachengue

A party, a big one.

Cacho

1. A chunk or piece of something, a bit of. "Un cacho de torta" = "A portion of cake".
2. Used sometimes in the opposite sense: "¡Qué cacho de jugador!" = "Wath a wonderful soccer player".

Cachucha

Vagina.

Cachuso (adj)

Someone or something ruined, old, worn-out, that works badly.

Cagar (v)

1. To do that something works badly.
2. To ruin projects, situations or relations.
3. To defraud someone, to cheat someone.
4. Used for to describe a superlative of an action:
—"Cagar a golpes" = "To give a lot of punchs to somebody"
—"Estar cagado" = "To be shat", which means to be very afraid, and also to be in very troubles.
—"Cagarse en las patas" = "To shit in your own legs", which means to be very afraid.
—"Cagarse de risa" = "To shit in laughs", which means to laugh a lot.
—"Estar cagado de frío" = "To be shat by cold weather", which means to be freezing.

(lit.) To defecate

Cagón

1. A coward, a fearful one.

2. A weak and sluggish person.
(Femenin: Cagona)

Cajeta
Vagina.

Calzado (adj)
Armed, carrying a weapon, especially a gun.
(lit.) Having footwear on.

Cana
1. A cup, a policeman.
2. Jail.

Cancha
Skill about something. "To have *cancha*" about something means to be an experimented guy in that area.

Canchereada
1. Brag, boast.
2. Swanking
See also: Fanfarronada.

Cancherear (v)
To do proper things of a *Canchero* (see).

Canchero
1. Smartass. One who pretend to know about everything —and really don't know so much about anything.
2. In some cases, someone who is experienced at something.

Caño

1. Joint.
2. Pipe for marijuana.
3. A gun (of a pickpocket).
4. Used in the popular phrase "Dar con un caño" ("Hit with a tube"), referred to a hard critic about someone.

(lit.) Tube.

Canuto (adj)

1. One who hides something.
2. Miser person.

Capo

1. As an adjective, means a great guy, who possesses many personal qualities.
2. The boss.

(lit.) from the Italian "capo" = the chief.

Careta (adj)

(Same for both genres)
1. Snobbish person, who claims more than he/she really is.
2. Person who doesn't consume drugs.

(lit.) Mask

Caretear (v)

1. To act unsincerely.
2. To claim or pretend for more.

Caripela

1. Face, but in a some ironical sense.
2. Sometimes it could be used for "ugly face"

Carucha
Face

Cascote (adj)
(Same for both genres)
One who is hard to understand or learn.
(lit.) Stone
See also: Ladrillo

Catrasca (adj)
(Same for both genres)
1. A very clumsy, awkward or stubborn person.
2. A disastrous person, who commits a mistake after other one.
3. Someone prosecuted by mishaps and heaviness. The word comes from "**Ca**gada **tras ca**gada" ("dung after dung").

Catrera
Bed.

Cebar (v)
To fill the cup of the infusion called *mate* (see).
(lit.) To bait.

Cepillar (v)
To fuck, to have sex. "Me la cepillé" ("I brushed her") = "I did have sex with her".
(lit.) To brush.

Chabomba
Women panties.
See also: Bombacha.

Chabón
Guy.

Chacón
Pussy, vagina.
(lit.) Shell.

Chacota
Take something "a la chacota" ("in the *chacota* way") means don't take it seriously.

Chamuyar (v)
1. To talk bullshit.
2. Try to cheat someone with false arguments.

Chamuyero (adj)
1. One who talks bullshit, sometimes with bad intentions.
2. A liar.

Chamuyo
Bullshit.

Chanchullo
1. Act of corruption, illicit agreement, dirty business.
2. Political maneuvers done in the dark.

Chanfle
Kicking the soccer ball with a curve effect.

Chanfleado (adj)
Twisted, curved, inclined, out of axis.

Changa

1. Temporary job.
2. Half-time job.

Changüí

An opportunity needed.

Chanta (adj)

(Same for both genres)
1. A chatterbox, a talkative
2. Someone who is capable of to cheat everyone to obtain advantages, in a sense a vagabond who doesn't want to work legally.
3. A shameless, an impertinent, a scoundrel, a sponger, a too much informal person
4. Someone who lives by tricking and lying, and almost against the law.
5. "Tirarse a chanta" ("To incline oneself to chanta") = This means to act with certain carelessness and laziness, when actually one might make it much better. Sadly, this concept describes certain dark side common to all the Argentinian people. Buenos Aires it's the "Kingdom of Could Be". Something like "Can you leave this for tomorrow? Well, then... why would you do it today?!".

Chantada

Everything which the *chanta* makes.
See: Chanta

Chapas

Used in the phrase "A las chapas" ("To sheet") in the sense of "to drive to too many speed".
(lit.) Metal sheet

Chapita (adj)

(Same for both genres)
Crazy. "Ella está *chapita*" = She's crazy.
(lit.) Little sheet.

Chata

A van.
(lit.) Flat

Chau

Bye!, goodbye!

Che

Exclamatory or nominal interjection, according to the case, used permanently and with a great variety of senses:
—As interjection, it means "Hey!" or "Hey, you!".
—Also used in the sense of *buddy*. "Vas a venir, che?" = "You will come, buddy?"; "¡Qué alegría verte, che!" = "Good to see you, man!".
—Used too as a meaningless interjection (no matter the context).

(lit.) Probably from the Mapuche word "che", which means "People". Mapuche people was a originary culture from the South of Argentine and Chile.

Cheto (adj)

Snobby. Person who pretend to be part of the High society. Stuck up.

China

Wife of the *gaucho* (see).

Chinche
Annoyance, ire, inconvenience, edginess.

Chinchudo (adj)
Nervous, angry, troublesome, irritated.

Chirimbolo
1. Tiny object, trifle, bauble.
2. Thing without very much value.

Chirola
Small change.

Chocho (adj)
Satisfied, glad, happy.

Chongo (adj)
Poor quality thing.

Chorro
1. Thief.
2. Also used in the sense of: Someone who doesn't deserve what he/she obtained, or that doesn't have merits enough to accede to the place that he/she tries to occupy.

Choto
1. Penis.
2. As an adjective: poor quality thing.

Chuchi
Girl of the working class when she's dressing to go out by night, generally with showy clothes, and in bad taste.

Chumbo

Gun, pistol.

Chupamedias (adj)

(Same for both genres)
Submissive and flattering person, that humbles himself easily.
(lit.) Sock-sucker

Chupar (v)

To drink wine, whisky or beer in great amounts.
(lit.) To sock.

Ciruja

Vagabond, beggar, bum.

Cloro

A piss.
(lit.) Chlorine (the element Cl)

Coco

Used in the sense of *loosing mind* in phrases like "Está *del coco*" ("He's *by his coconut*"), which means "He's crazy".
(lit.) Coconut.
See also: Peluca, Gorra, Tomate, Bonete.

Coger (v)

To fuck, to have sex.
(lit.) To clutch.

Colgado (adj)

Absent-minded, thoughtful.

Colgar (v)

1. To resign, to give up (a job, or a situation, or relationship)
2. *Colgarse* (reflexive verb): To remain thoughtful, in a reflexive mood, absent-minded.

(lit.) To hang.

Combustible

Alcohol, an intake of an alcoholic drink.

(lit.) Fuel.

Comer (v)

1. *Comerse* (reflexive verb): make the sexual act to somebody.
2. "Comerse la cabeza" ("Eat the own head") = Be really worry about something.
3. "Comerse un garrón" (Eat a bummer") = To suffer a disappointment, or an unfair situation.

(lit.) To eat.

Comilón

Gay guy.

(lit.) Big eater.

Concha

1. Pussy, vagina.
2. It's also used as a part of an insult: "¡La concha de tu hermana!" = "For your sister's vagina!"

(lit.) Shell.

Conchuda

Bad woman, complicated woman.

(lit.) Woman with a big vagina.

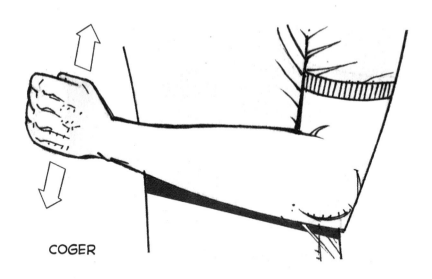

COGER

Copado (adj)
Cool person.

Cornudo (adj)
Person whose couple has sex with other people.
(lit.) Cuckold

Cortado
An expresso coffee, with a touch of warm milk.
(lit) Cutted.

Cotorra
1. Pussy, vagina.
2. Chatterbox (referred to women).
(lit.) Parrot.

Crepar (v)
To pass away.

Cualquiera
Used as an exclamation, with the same sense of *Whatever*.

Cuernos
"Meter los cuernos" ("To put the horns") it's to cheat your husband or wife, having sex with other people.
(lit.) Horns

Cuero
"Sacar el cuero" ("Take out the skin") means to talk badly or to gossip about some absent person.
(lit.) Leather

Culear (v)
To have sex, to fornicate.

Culo
Good luck. "¡Qué culo!" = "What a good luck!".
(lit.) Ass.

Culos de botella
A pair of glasses with very thick lenses.
(lit.) Bottle bottoms.

Currar (v)
1. To defraud, to scam.
2. To obtain many earnings by little effort or immoral attitudes.

Curro

1. Fraud.
2. "Buen curro" (Good *curro*) = a very convenient job or business, be legal or not so much.

Cursi (adj)

(Same for both genres)
Pretentious, twee, affected.
See also: Tilingo.

Curtir (v)

1. "Curtir con alguien" (*Curtir* with somebody) = To have sex with somebody.
2. To use, to be involved in, or to take part of something: "Él curtió mucho comunismo" = "He'd take part of many communist activities"; "Ella curtió mucho boliche" = "She used to go to the pubs frequently"

Denso (adj)

Heavy, unbearable, troublesome person, who bores to everyone.
(lit.) Thick.

Desbole

Big disorder, in all senses.
See also: Despelote, Quilombo.

Despelote

A big disorder, a mess.
See also: Desbole, Quilombo.

Dibujado (adj)

1. Amazed, bewildered, stoned by a surprising situation or something that anyone said.

2. To feel left out in a situation.

(lit.) Drawn

See also: Pintado.

Diego

10%: Commission or percentage of profit obtained by some kind of corrupt or illegal transaction. The word comes from the similarity between the male name "Diego" and the word "Diez" (Ten).

Embocar (v)

To catch someone in many senses: discover anyone in a suspicious situation, discover someone cheating, lay a trap successfully.

Embole

Very boring situation.

See also: Empelote.

Empelote

Something very boring.

See also: Desbole, Quilombo.

Enganchar (v)

—"Enganchar a alguien" ("To hook up someone") = To get a date with someone.

—To get involved in a situation.

(lit.) To hook up

Engranar (v)

To become angry.

(lit.) To mesh.

Engrupir (v)

To fool someone, usually by using nice words.

Enroscar (v)

To induce and involve someone in order that he/she takes part of some unclear situation. To convince someone with sinuous arguments.

(lit.) To screw in.

Escabiar (v)

To drink alcohol: wine, beer, vodka, etc.

Escabio

Any alcoholic drinks: wine, whisky, beer, vodka, etc.

Escrachar (v)

To uncover in public, to show in public that someone as having an illegal or evil behaviour.

Escracho (adj)

(Same for both genres)
Ugly and/or dirty persone.

Facha

Elegance, quality of a good looking person. "¡Qué facha!" = "What a good looking guy !".

Fachero (adj)

Someone who has good presence.

Facho
Person with fascist ideas, a Nazi.
(lit.) From the Italian fascista.

Falopa
Any illegal drugs: marijuana, cocaine, heroine, etc.

Falopero (adj)
Drug addict.

Fanfarrón (adj)
Boastful, swanky.
(Femenine: Fanfarrona)

Fanfarronada
1. Brag, boast.
2. Swanking

See also: Canchereada

Faso
1. Cigarette.
2. Joint.

Feca
Expresso coffee.

Fiaca
Laziness, idleness, constant desires of leisure. But "fiaca" is not something that you *feel*, but something that you *make*, an active decision of do nothing.

PARA CHUPARSE LOS DEDOS

Fiambre

Dead body, corpse.
(lit.) Served cold.

Fifar (v)

To have sex, to fuck.

Fija

1. An information or idea absolutely trustworthy.
2. As interjection, means "For sure!".

Finiquitar (v)
1. To finish off a matter, to close an issue properly.
2. To die, to end, to be through.

Fisurado (adj)
Exhausted, extremely tired
(lit.) Fissured.

Flashear (v)
Be astonished, to remain amazed.
(lit.) derived from the English word "flash".

Forro
1. Condom.
2. A fool, a dummy.

Forrear
To treat someone badly in a consistent way, especially in public.
See also: Basurear.

Franela
Action of *franelear* (see).

Franelear
To do caresses and kiss someone, with a strongly erotic sense.
See also: Transa.

Fulero (adj)
1. Ugly person.
2. Hard situation.

Full

1. "Estar a full" ("To be full") = To be very busy (a person) or completely full (a place, like in English language)
2. As an interjection: "¡A full!" ("Fully" !) means "Absolutely!".

Fusilado (adj)

1. Very tired.
2. Depressed.

Gaita

Spanish man.

(lit.) Bag-pipe.

Gallego

Spanish man (from "galician", inhabitant of Galicia, one of the Spanish provinces, from where came most of the immigrants in the early 20th century).

Gamba

1. "Hacer la gamba" ("Make *gamba* to someone") = To help, to accompany and to support someone.
2. "Meter la gamba" ("To put the leg") = To make a big mistake.
3. 100 pesos, dollars or any legal tender.

(lit.) from the Italian word for "leg".

Garca

(Same for both genres)
Swindler, bad person, one who defrauds or cheats other people.

Garcha

1. Penis
2. Thing without value.
3. Very low quality thing.

Garchar (v)
To have sex, to fuck.

Gardel
—To say to someone "¡Sos Gardel!" ("You're Gardel!") is like say to him that he's the best, the greatest. It means something like "You're the one!" or "You're at the top!".
—"¡Andá a cantarle a Gardel!" ("Let's go to sing for Gardel!") = "To hell with you", "What it's wrong with you ?", "Fuck off !".
(lit.) The word comes from the famous Tango singer Carlos Gardel.

Garrón
1. An unfair situation for someone, a bummer.
2. Used habitually in the expression "Comerse un garrón" (Eat a bummer"), which means "To suffer a big disappointment".

Garronear (v)
To ask for money, to beg.

Garronero (adj)
Person who always ask for money or anything, a sponger.
See also: Manguero, Pedigüeño

Gatillar (v)
Pay the bill (in any case).
(lit.) To pull the trigger

Gato
A whore, a prostitute.
(lit.) Cat.

Gauchada

A personal favour.

(lit.) Literally it means "Something that a gaucho does"; the gaucho (see) was typically considered attentive and helpful.

Gaucho

Rural worker, similar to the USA cowboy.

Gil

A fool, a dummy.

Goma

A woman's breast.

Gorra

Used in the sense of *loosing mind* in phrases like "Está *del bonete*" ("He's *by his cap*"), which means "He's crazy".

(lit.) Cap.

See also: Coco, Bonete, Peluca, Tomate.

Grasa (adj)

(Same for both genres)

Person, place or habit that totally lacks of refinement, subtlety or quality.

(lit.) Greasy.

Groncho (adj)

1. Contemptuous word for "half-breed"
(Note: at Buenos Aires, "Negro" it's the word used for the people who has mix of American native race, but this people do

not have anything in common with the black people from Afrika).
2. "Grasa" (see)

Grosso (adj)
1. A very important person (in society, political, arts, etc.)
2. Someone who is very respected in what he/she does.

Guacho (adj)
1) Used as an insult, it's very hard, like "son of a bitch".
2) Also used used as admiring exclamation: "¡Qué guacho!", in various senses like "Great job, Well done, You're the best".
(lit.) Orphan.

Guampas
"Meter las guampas" ("To put the horns") it's to cheat your husband or wife, having sex with other people. It's exactly the same for "Meter los cuernos" (see "Cuernos").

Guampudo (adj)
Person whose couple has sex with other people.
See also: Cornudo

Guarangada
Rude and obscene expression.

Guarango (adj)
Badly educated person, rude, who uses rude and obscene words.
See also: Guaso.

Guaso (adj)
A rude person.
See also: Guarango

Guita
Money, cash.

Guitarrear (v)
To speak senseless, to speak without going to the point ever.
(lit.) To play guitar.

Hostia
Something "de la hostia" ("like the *hostia*") means something really big and great, including abstract things as talent or intelligence.
(lit.) Eucharistic wafer.

Huevada
1. Thing that doesn't matter, things without very much value.
2. A stupid idea.

Huevón (adj)
An idiot, a fool.
(lit.) Big egg.
See also: Boludo, Pelotudo
(Femenine: Huevona)

Huevos
1. Testicles.
2. In that sense, "Tener huevos" ("To have eggs") means be a brave person.
(lit.) Eggs.

Hugo ("to call Hugo")
"Llamar a Hugo" ("call Hugo") = To vomit because of a drunkenness. The proper name Hugo, pronounced gutturally, seems the sound of a person vomiting.

Jabón

A fright.
(lit.) Soap.

Jamón

Used in the exclamative phrase "¡Jamón del medio!" ("Central part of a piece of boiled ham"), with the sense of "What a beautiful woman" or in general "What a special thing".
(lit). Ham.

Joda

1. Joke, kidding, non-serious things said or done.
2. Party, organized fun, a house party.
3. "Irse de joda" = Going out to get fun.
4. The word also have the opposite sense: a bad situation.

Joder (v)

1. To make a joke to someone.
2. Hang out and have fun.
3. To screw up, to ruin the chances of something

Jovato (adj)

1. Old, aged person, elder.
2. Someone that, being a young person yet, has attitudes of aged person.

Joya

Exclamative expression for "Great", "Marvelous", and in some cases just for "Ok".
(lit.) Jewel .

Junar (v)
1. To look to something.
2. To know.

Laburar (v)
To work.
(lit.) Comes from the Italian lavorare.

Laburo
Job.
(lit.) Comes from the Italian lavoro.

Lacra (adj)
(Same for both genres)
1. An outsider. Someone who lives out of the society, who is out of the financial and social system.
2. Also used to refer to delinquents.

Ladrillo (adj)
One who is hard to understand or learn.
(lit.) Brick
See also: Cascote

Langa
A very ladiesman.

Larva (adj)
(Same for both genres)
Lazy and scrounger person, who does not do anything by himself.
(lit.) Larva.

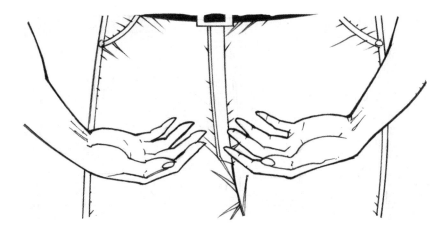

CON LOS HUEVOS LLENOS

Lastrar (v)
To eat.

Leche
1. Semen, spooge.
2. Attitude or predisposition, and also luck, fortune. It's ised accompanied by the qualifiers "good" (buena leche) or "bad" (mala leche).
(lit.) Milk.

Lenteja (adj)
(Same for both genres)
1. Slow and awkward person, of slow reactions.
2. Person who has comprehension and learning problems.
(lit.) Lentil.

Leones
Pants, trousers.
(lit.) Lions.

Levantar (v)
To seduce successfully someone, to get a date with.
(lit.) To raise

Lienzo
Pants, trousers.
(lit.) Canvas.

Ligar (v)
1. To receive good cards in a game.
2. To receive a hard punishment.

Lija
Hunger.
—"Tengo una lija…!" ("What a sandpaper I have…!") = "I'm starving"
—"Pasar lija" ("To traverse a sandpaper") or "Correr la lija" ("Run behind the sandpaper") = To have money troubles and cannot eat enough because of it.
(lit.) Sandpaper

Limado (adj)
Someone diminished in his mental skill and his physical shape. It also refers to the results of drugs abuse.
(lit.) Filed.

Loco

Used as "buddy" or "man" (from the Hippie culture of the 70s).
(lit.) Crazy.

Lolas

Woman's breasts.

Lomo

1. A perfect shape (in men)
2. A beautiful and hot body (in women)

(lit.) Loin.

Lompa

Pants, trousers.

Lorca

Warm or hot weather.

Luca

1,000 dollars, or 1.000 pesos, or same amount of any country' legal tender.

Lungo (adj)

A tall person.

Macana

Error, mistake.

Macanudo (adj)

1. Terrific, great.
2. A good and nice person.

Maconia
Marijuana.

Mal Bicho (adj)
(Same for both genres)
Very bad person.

Malco (adj)
(Same for both genres)
Habitually used about women, refers to someone who is in a bad mood for be sexually unsatisfied. Comes from "***Mal co***gido".

Mamado (adj)
Drunk person.

Mamar (v)
1. To practise a fellatio.
2. *Mamarse* (reflexive verbe): to get drunk.
(lit.) To suckle.

Mambo
Mind trouble, psychological trauma, condition of confusion.
(lit.) Comes from mambo, an Afro-American rhythm.

Mamerto (adj)
Fool, idiot.

Manducar (v)
To eat.

MAMADO

Mango
1. Peso (Argentinian legal tender).
2. "Estar al mango" ("To be at the mango") = Be in full capacities, going to full speed.

Manguear (v)
To ask for money, to beg.

Manguero (adj)
Person who always ask for money or anything, a sponger.
See also: Garronero, Pedigüeño.

Manyar
1. To know.
2. To eat.
(lit.) from the Italian mangiare (to eat).

Marica

A gay man.

Masa

"Dar masa" ("To give dough") = Make the sexual act furiously, ardently.

(lit.) Dough.

Mate

Traditional beverage of Argentina. It's an infusion of *yerba mate* (*Ilex paraguayiensis*), an herb from Argentine and Paraguay. It's served in a little wooden or metal teacup (traditionally, a decorative gourd), and it's drunk using a special metal straw called *bombilla*.

Matina

The morning.

Maza

Terrific, great. "Es una maza" ("He/she/it is a sledge-hammer") = "Is the best".

(lit.) Sledge hammer.

Metejón

A passion for an object, person or issue; a strong yearning.

Mierda

Used in the phrase "Hecho mierda" ("I'm a piece of shit") with various senses: I'm broken, I'm exhausted, I'm depressed, I'm really bad.

(lit.) Shit.

Milico
Military man.

Milonga
Variation of Tango music, which have a faster rhythm.

Milonguear (v)
To dance the Tango, and in general go to dance at night clubs.

Mina
Girl.

Minga
Exclamative word for "No way" or "Fuck you".

Mishadura
Bad economic situation, economic crisis, recession, lack of opportunities for employment and trade.

Moco
Big mistake.
(lit.) Mucus, snot.

Mongui (adj)
(Same for both genres)
Idiot. The word come from "mogólico", which means "person with Down syndrome".

Morfar (v)
To eat, but not just the action. "Morfar" also implies the pleasure of enjoying the luncheon and the dinner surrounded by friends, and also certain forms of gastronomic ceremony.

Morfi
Food

Morocho (adj)
Dark haired person.

Morondanga
A poor quality object.

Mortal
Superb, excellent.

Mosca
Cash, money.
(lit.) Fly (insect)

Mufa
1. "Have *mufa*" means to be in a dark mood.
2. Someone that brings bad luck to the others.
3. A bad foreboding.

Musarela
As an exclamative expression, means "Be quiet!", "Silence!".
(lit.) Comes from the Italian word mozzarella, a kind of cheese.

Nabo (adj)
Fool, idiot.
(lit.) Turnip.

Napia
Nose.

Naranja
Nothing. "No pasa naranja" = "Nothing happens".
(lit.) Orange.

Naso
Nose.

Ñoqui
Someone who receives a salary without going to work, because of an arrangement related to the political corruption
(lit.) Comes from the Italian word gnocci, *a kind of* pasta.

Ojete
1. Arse.
2. Good luck. "¡Qué ojete!" = "What a good luck!".

Onda
1. "Buena onda": something cool.
2. "De onda": to do something for helping anyone, to do a favor.
3. "Con onda": to do something in a funny mood.
4. "Tirar onda": to make sexual insinuations.

(lit.) Wave.

Orto
1. Arse.
2. Good luck.
3. "Tener cara de orto" ("To have a face that seems an anus") = To be upset and looks very angry.
4. "La loma del orto" ("The Anus' Hill") = Nowhere; a very distant place.

Otario
Jerk, stupid.

Pachanga
Big party, with so much fun and dance.

Pachanguear (v)
Go to the party, have fun in a party.

Pachorra
Laziness, idleness, desires of leisure.

Pachorriento (adj)
Person who shows always *pachorra* (see).

Paisano
Member of the Argentinian-Jewish community.

Paja
1. Masturbation
2. Laziness, lack of strength, tendency to avoid work and effort.

Pajero (adj)
1. A jerkoff, someone who does nothing productive.
2. One that practises so much the masturbation.

Palo
—1.000.000 pesos, or same amount of any country' legal tender.
—"Palo Verde": 1,000,000 dollars.
—"Estar al palo" ("To be at the *palo*") = To have an erection.

Pancho
A hot dog, Argentine style. Often sold in street stands.

Papear (v)
To speak senseless, to speak without going to the point ever.

Papelón
Embarrassing situation.
(lit.) A great paper ("papel" -"paper"- it's the Spanish for "role in a play").

Papo
Pretentious and senseless speech.

Paquete
Penis and testicles that seems a package under the pants.
(lit.) package
See also: Bulto.

Paragua
Contemptuous word for "Paraguayan people".
(lit.) Umbrella.

Parir (v)
To spend big difficulties to solve a situation.
(lit.) To give birth.

Patota
A group of violent people, especially any group of young mobbers who bother people in the street, threatens them and/or rob them, or a group of fans of a football team before or after a match, etc.

Patotero (adj)

Mobber, member of a *patota* (see).

Patovica

Person who guards the access to discos, clubs, etc., and/or are in charge of taking drunkards and discriminated minorities out; often associated with gym-trained, medication-enhanced muscular types.

Pava

The specific kettle for to boil the water for make the mate.

Pedigüeño (adj)

Person who always ask for money or anything, a sponger.

See also: Garronero, Manguero.

Pedo

1. A drunkenness.
2. Used in expressions like:

—"Al pedo" ("In fart") = To haven't nothing to do / Useless.

—"Estar en pedo" ("To be at Fart") = To be drunk, to be pissed, be sloshed.

—"Ponerse en pedo" ("Put into Fart") = To get drunk, to get pissed, get sloshed.

—"Estar al pedo" (To be in fart") = To haven't nothing to do.

— Exclamative expression: "¡Estás en pedo!" = "You must be kidding!" / "No way!".

—"Vivir en una nube de pedo" ("To live inside a fart cloud") = To be a person without worries, but in a situation for which you should worry.

— "Cagar a pedos" ("To shit in farts") = To give a strong verbal rebuke to someone.

— "De pedo" ("By fart") = By chance, just accidentally or casually.

(lit.) Fart.

Pedorro (adj)
Bad quality thing, or object, or even an idea.

Pejerto (adj)
Fool, idiot.

Película
"Hacerse la película" ("Make your own movie") means to worry about a situation that it's not completely real.
(lit.) Movie.

Pelota / Pelotas
1. One of the words for *testicles*.
2. It's used in many senses, according at the moment or situation. A few exemples:
—In the sense of *pay attention*: "Dame pelota" ("Give me ball") = Pay attention to me; "Nadie le da pelota" ("Nobody gives ball to him") = Nobody pay attention to him.
—In the sense of *annoying*: "Me rompe las pelotas" ("She breaks my balls") = She really upsets me.
—In the sense of *boring*: "Tu amigo me hincha las pelotas" ("Your friend fills my balls"" = Your friend really boring me.
—In the sense of *something that lacks*: "Estoy en pelotas" ("I'm in my balls") = I don't have anything, *or* I don't know anything about this subject, *or* I'm haven't nothing to protect me.
—In the sense of *nudity:* "Estoy en pelotas" ("I'm in my balls") = I'm naked.
(lit.) Ball, Balls
See also: Bola / Bolas.

Pelotudo
1. Fool, silly, asshole.
2. "Hacerse el pelotudo" ("Play the fool") means "To pretend mis-

understand" for to take advantage of a situation: "Se hace el pelotudo" ("He plays the fool").
(lit.) One with big testicles.
See also: Boludo.

Peluca
Used in the sense of *loosing mind* in phrases like "Está *de la peluca*" ("He's *by his wig*)", which means "He's crazy".
(lit.) Wig.
See also: Coco, Gorra, Tomate, Bonete.

Pendejada
Action, behavior or reaction proper of a teenager, and obviously improper for an adult person.

Pendejo
1. Pubic hair.
2. Teenager.

Pendorcho
Any sort of small object, generally a simple mechanical part that is or should appear protruding from a larger object.

Pepa
A dose of LSD.

Percha
Used in the phrase "Hecho percha" ("I'm a coat hanger") with various senses: I'm broken, I'm exhausted, I'm depressed, I'm really bad.
(lit.) Hanger.

Peroncho

Contemptuous word for "member of the Peronism" (see).

Peronism

An Argentine political movement based on the ideas and programs associated with former President Juan Perón and his second wife, spiritual leader of the movement: Eva Perón, "Evita".

Peronista

(Same for both genres)
Person who sympathizes with Peronism (see).

Peruca

(Same for both genres)
Contemptuous word for "member of the Peronism" (see).

Pesado (adj)

1. Annoying, boring.
2. Person or situation dangerous or hard to carry on, hard to handle. (Note: *in this sense, teenagers and middle-age people also uses the English word* heavy)

(lit.) Heavy.

Pescado (adj)

(Same for both genres)
1. Fool, asshole.
2. Ingenuous person, easy to cheat.

(lit.) Fish.

Pesto

1. Traditional sauce from Genova (Italy), used for *pasta*. Very popular in Buenos Aires.

EN PAMPA Y LA VÍA

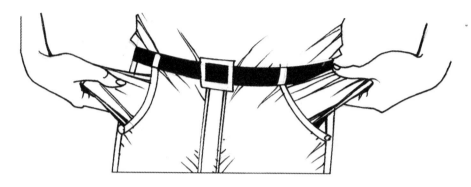

2. "Dar el pesto": To win a match (soccer, etc.) for a large advantage.

Pete
Fellatio.

Petear (v)
To perform oral sex on somebody.

Petera (adj)
A woman who habitually performs oral sex on men. Occasionally used in the masculine form, "Petero" referred to a gay man who performs oral sex to another guy.

Petiso (adj)
Short, of small stature.

Pibe
Kid.

Pifiada
Big mistake.

Pifiar (v)
To make a big mistake.

Pijotear (v)
To act in an avaricious way.

Pijotero (adj)
A mean person.

Pilas
Referred to the personal energy, to the personal push. "Ponete las pilas" ("Put your batteries on") = "Go on !", "Move on, man !"

(lit.) Batteries.

Pilchas
Clothes.

Pinta
Elegance, quality of a good looking person. "¡Qué pinta!" = "What a good looking guy !".

Pintado (adj)
1. To remain amazed, surprised by a situation.
2. To feel yourself left out in a situation.

(lit.) Painted

See also: Dibujado.

Pintar (v)

To appear an opportunity, to come up a profitable situation.
(lit.) To paint.

Pinturita

Perfect, sharp, squeaky clean, in very fine condition.
(lit.) Little picture.

Piola (adj)

(Same for both genres)
1. A smart and crafty person.
2. "Quedarse piola" ("To stay *piola*) = To remain calm, to stay apart of a situation.

Pipón (adj)

To be satisfied after having eaten so much.
(Femenine: Pipona)

Piquetero

A person, generally unemployed or sub-employed, that participates in *piquetes* (a gathering of such people, usually blocking some important way and demonstrating) to protest his/her condition.

Pirado (adj)

Crazy, mad.

Pirar (v)

To go mad. To become crazy.

Pirucho (adj)

Crazy, mad.

Pirulo
A year (used only as a unit for people's age).

Plomo
(Same for both genres)
1. Someone or something annoying, boring.
2. Bullet
(lit.) Lead.

Pocilga
Dirty and miserable room or house.

Polvo
1. Ejaculation.
2. Sexual act.
(lit.) Dust. From the Biblical quote "Ashes to ashes, dust to dust".

Ponja
Japanese man.

Pornoco
Furuncle that grew, according to a popular belief, due to having had no sex for long time. The word comes from "Por no coger" ("Because having no sex").

Poronga
1. Penis
2. Thing or idea that is really unuseful, bad quality object.

Porongo
1. Penis
2. Teacup for mate infusion, a pumpkin-made cup used only in the North of the country.

Porro
Joint, marijuana cigarette.

Porrón
A little bottle of beer.

Porteño (adj)
Person who was born in Buenos Aires. The word comes from "Puerto" ("Port"), and literally means "Inhabitant of the port".

Posta
1. The real truth about something.
2. As an exclamation: "¡Posta!" = "Seriusly !", "I mean it !".

Pucho
Cigarette.

Putear (V)
1. To insult.
2. To use rude language.

Quichicientos
It's a ficticious number: large number, a lot, a gazillion.

Quilombero (adj)
Troublemaker.

Quilombo
1. A disorder, a chaotic and untidy situation.
2. A brothel.

Rajar (v)

To flee, to escape, to run, to hurry up.

(lit.) To split.

Rascar (v)

Used as a reflexive verb: "Rascarse" ("To scracht yourself") means to do nothing at all. Another expressions with the same sense: "Rascarse las bolas" or "Rascarse las pelotas" ("To scratch your own balls").

(lit.) To scratch.

Rati

1. A cup, a policeman.

Raviol

Cocaine dose, a tiny bag of cocaine.

(lit.) From "ravioli", an Italian dish: squares of pasta dough with a filling.

Rebotar (v)

1. To reject, to return, to give back for review: "Me rebotaron el pedido de crédito" = "They rejected my credit application".
2. To bounce, to be rejected, to be returned: "El cheque rebotó" = "The check was bounced".
3. To be rejected by somebody one has sexually advanced on.

(lit.) To bounce, to bounce off.

Reverendo (adj)

Used as an emphatic mark in insults, as in "Reverendo hijo de puta" = "You Reverend son of a bitch". Because it sounds like the ecclesiastical title, it lends importance to the rest of the phrase.

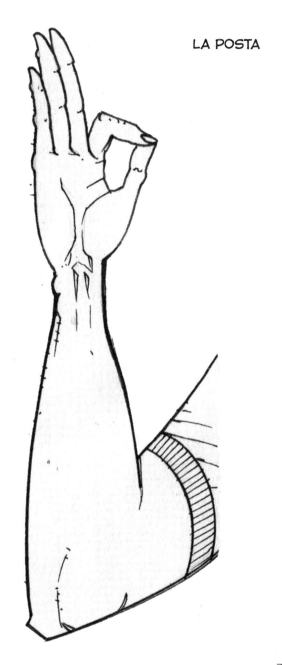

LA POSTA

Rolinga (adj)

(Same for both genres)
Fan of The Rolling Stones, generally from the working classes, who dresses symbols as the famous red tongue, t-shirts with images related to the band, Jagger's early times hair cut-like, etc.

Ruso

Jewish man.

(lit.) Russian man.

Sacado (adj)

Person that shows a condition of great mental excitation, as if all reason had been extracted out of mind.

(lit.) Taken off.

Salame (adj)

(Same for both genres)
Stupid, dummy.

(lit.) From Italian: salame, *traditional cured sausage from Italy, very popular in Buenos Aires.*

Sanata

Speech that is characterized for being exaggerated, affected, recherché and essentially fraudulent.

Sanatero (adj)

Liar. Person who makes *Sanata* (ver).

Sobre

Bed. "Irse al sobre" ("Go to the envelope") = "Go to bed", "To hick the sack".

(lit.) Envelope.

Sopapo

1. Slap.
2. Punch.

Sope

Peso (Argentinian legal tender). Comes from "Peso" saying backwards.

Sorete

1. Piece of shit, arse biscuits.
2. Bad person.

Sota

1. The ten card in a Spanish deck; used figuratively in the phrase "Se le cayó una sota" ("To drop a ten-spot") = "To lie grossly about one's age".
2. "Hacerse el sota" ("To pretend be a *sota*"): to hide oneself, to make oneself unnoticed, to pretend one's got nothing to do with things.

Tacaño

Stingy, mean, miser.

Tacho

1. Taxi cab.
2. Ass, especially a big one.

Taco

1. "Echar un taco" ("Throw out a taco) = Have sex, in general; more specifically: to ejaculate.
2. "Al taco" ("Up to the *taco*) = In full capacities, plenty of energy.
(lit.) Heel (of shoes).

Tanga

1. Fraud, deception.
2. Women panties.

Tano

Italian man.

Tapera

1. A very humble house.
2. Any place in ruins and abandoned.

Tarro

Good luck.

Tela

Money.

Telo

A by-the-hour motel.

Tilingo (adj)

Pretentious, twee, affected.
See also: Cursi.

Timba

A place for gambling.

Timbear

To bet for money.

Timbero (adj)
A gambler.

Timbos
Shoes.

Tipo
Guy.
(lit.) Type.

Tocado (adj)
Slightly crazy, or a bit drunk.
(lit.) Touched.

Tomate
Used in the sense of loosing mind in phrases like "Está *del bonete*" ("He's by his tomato"), which means "He's crazy".
(lit.) Tomato.
See also: Coco, Gorra, Bonete, Peluca.

Tongo
Fraud, swindle (especially in contest or games).

Toque
1. A bit of.
2. "Al toque" ("In touch") = Instantaneously.
3. "Al toque" ("In touch") = Nearby.
(lit.) Touch

Tordo
Medical doctor. Comes from "Doctor" saying backwards.

Tornillo

Cold weather.

(lit.) Screw.

Torta

Lesbian.

(lit.) Cake.

Tortillera

Lesbian.

Traba

A transvestite man who works as a whore.

Trabuco

A transvestite man who works as a whore.

Tragaleche (adj)

(Same for both genres)
1. A man or a woman who drinks semen after performing fellatio
2. A male homosexual.

(lit.) Milk swallower.

See also: Tragasable.

Tragasable (adj)

(Same for both genres)
1. A homosexual man
2. Occasionally also applied to a woman with a strong sexual desire for males.

(lit.) Sword eater.

See also: Tragaleche.

Tranca
A drunkenness.

Transa
A deal, a contract or an agreement against the law.

Transar (v)
1. To make love, to caress, to kiss.
2. To make a deal, a contract or an agreement against the law.

Transero (adj)
Person who makes deals, contracts or agreements against the law.

Traste
Ass.

Travesaño
A transvestite man who works as a whore.

Trincar (v)
To fuck, to have sex.

Trola
1. Whore, prostitute.
2. A promiscuos woman.

Trolo
A gay man.

Trompa
Mouth.

Trompada
Punch in the very mouth.

Trucha
Face.

Truchada
1. Something that is or has been made trucho (see).
2. A fake, a bad-quality forge.

Trucho (adj)
1. Fake.
2. False.
3. Poor quality thing.

Tubazo
Telephone call.

Tubo
1. Telephone
2. Big muscles.

(lit.) Tube.

Turco
Arabian (thing, person)

(lit.) Turkish.

Turro
A bad, evil, obnoxious, or deceiving person.

Vaquita
The action and result of collecting money among friends, workmates, etc., especially in small amounts, to buy something that the group or one of its members needs.
(lit.) Little cow.

Verde
Dollar.
(lit.) Green.

Yanqui
North-American man.

Yapa
A free adition, a small quantity that someone adds to the real value of something that you bought, as a form of comity. Used for money (a tip), weight or quantity.

Yeta
1. Someone or something with bad luck.
2. Someone or something that brings bad luck to the others.

Yoni
Englishman, North-American man.
(lit.) Comes from Argentinian pronunciation of Johnny.

Yonki
Junkie: Drug addict (from Spain, with some use in Buenos Aires)

TENÉS QUIKI

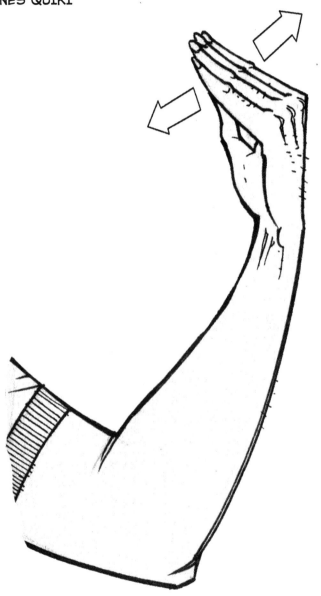

Yuta
Police (as institution).

Zafar (v)
1. To save yourself from some troubled or dangerous situation.
2. To achieve something in a way just correct, just acceptable, not great but ok.

Zafarrancho
Great disorder, mess situation.

Zarpado (adj)
1. As interjection: "¡Zarpado!" = "Cool !", in the same sense of "¡Bárbaro!" (see).
2. Wild person.

Zarpar
Used as a reflexive verb: "Zarparse" = To go beyond the limits.

Zolcillonca
Man's underwear. Comes from "Calzoncillo" saying backwards

Zoquete
Fool, dummy

Zurdo
Person with socialist or communist ideas.
(lit.) Left handed.

Part 2

A brief English-Argentinian guide

In this section, you can search for many habitually used words of the Buenos Aires slang . But this is only a guide, for which, to have a more wide information about every word, you will have to look for in the main section of this book.

A bit
Cacho

A lot
Bocha

Absent-minded
Colgado – Dibujado – Pintado

Ass
Culo – Ojete – Orto

Asshole / Fool / Dummy / Silly / Idiot / Stupid
Boludo – Pelotudo – Forro – Gil – Aparato – Huevón – Lenteja – Limado – Otario – Pejerto – Pescado – Salame – Nabo

Bad lucky people
Catrasca – Yeta

Bad mood
Bajón

Bad people
Bicho – Mal bicho – Chanta – Conchuda (for women) – Garca – Guacho – Lacra – Turro

Bad smell
Baranda

Bathroom
Biorsi

Bed
Catrera – Sobre

Boring people
Pesado – Plomo – Denso – *Heavy*

Boring situation
Embole – Empelote

Bum
Ciruja

Bus
Bondi

Cheap, cheesy
Berreta – Chongo – Choto – Grasa

Cheapskate
Amarrete – Pijotero – Tacaño

Clothes
Pilchas

Clumsy / Awkward / Stubborn
Catrasca

Condom
Forro

Cool people
Capo – Copado

Coward
Cagón

Crazy
Loco – Pirado – Pirucho – Chapita – Tocado – Sacado – Abollado – Tocado

Crazy situation / Disorder
Bardo – Quilombo – Bolonqui – Desbole – Despelote – Barullo

Drinks / To drink
Birra (beer) – Porrón (bottle of beer) – Escabio (any alcoholic drink) – Chupar (to drink) – Escabiar (to drink) – Pedo (drunkenness) – Tranca (drunkenness)

Drugs
Blanca (cocaine) – Faso (joint) – Porro (joint) – Caño (joint) – Maconia (marijuana) – Raviol (cocaine dose) – Falopa (any drug) – Falopero (addict)

Face
Caripela – Trucha – Carucha

Fake
Trucho

Food
Morfi (in general) – Bife (beefsteack)

Funny guy
Banana

Gay guy
Marica – Trolo – Comilón

Girl
Mina

Glad
Chocho

Good looking Persons
Bombón – Fachero – Langa

Great, Terrific
Bárbaro – Brutal – Macanudo – Maza

Gun, Pistol
Caño – Chumbo

Guy
Chabón – Loco – Tipo

Head
Bocho – Coco

Informer
Batidor – Batilana – Alcahuete – Botón – Buchón

Job
Laburo – Changa – Curro

Kid
Pibe – Borrego – Pendejo

Lawyer
Ave Negra

Laziness
Fiaca – Pachorra

Lazy
Atorrante – Larva

Lesbian
Bombero – Tortillera – Torta

Luck
Culo – Ojete – Orto

Mistake / Big mistake
Pifiada – Macana – Moco

Money
Chirola (small change) – Diego (10%) – Mango (1) – Gamba (100) – Luca (1,000) – Palo (1,000,000) – Peso (legal tender) – Guita (in general) – Mosca (in general) – Tela (in general) – Verde (dollar)

No way!
¡Minga!

Ok!
Bárbaro

Pants / Trousers
Lienzos – Leones

Party
Pachanga – Cachengue

Penis
Banana – Bulto – Choto – Garcha – Poronga – Paquete

Policeman, Cup
Botón – Cana – Rati – Yuta

Robbery
Afano

Rude people
Guarango – Guaso

Ruined, worn-out
Cachuso

Smart
Bocho – Piola

Smartass
Canchero – Fanfarrón

Snobbish person
Careta – Cheto

Sponger
Manguero – Garronero – Pedigüeño

Stupid thing and/or Object without value
Boludez – Pelotudez – Chirimbolo – Morondanga – Pedorro

Testicles
Huevos – Bolas – Pelotas

Thief
Chorro

Tired
Fisurado – Fusilado – Baqueteado

To bribe
Aceitar

To cheat
Abrochar – Cagar – Chamuyar – Embocar – Currar – Engrupir – Enroscar

To cheat on (sexually)
Meter los cuernos ("To put the horns")
Meter las guampas ("To put the horns")
Cornudo (who has been cheated on)

To date
Enganchar – Levantar

To die
Crepar

To eat
Morfar – Lastrar – Manducar – Manyar

To finance
Bancar

To fuck / To have sex
Coger – Fifar – Garchar – Trincar – Cepillar – Comerse – Culear – Curtir – Polvo (ejaculation) – Pete (fellatio)

To sleep
Apolillar

To steal
Afanar

To support (a friend, etc.)
Bancar

Transvestite
Traba – Trabuco – Travesaño

Ugly person
Bagayo – Bicho – Escracho – Fulero

Vagina
Concha – Cachucha – Cajeta – Chacón – Cotorra

Weird
Bizarro

Whatever
¡Cualquiera!

Whore
Puta – Trola – Gato – Atorranta

Woman breasts
Gomas – Lolas

Woman panties
Bombacha – Chabomba

Otros títulos de nuestra editorial

VÁYANSE TODOS A LA MIERDA, DIJO CLINT EASTWOOD

Néstor Barron

320 páginas
14 x 23 cm
ISBN: 978-950-754-235-0

"Lo bueno de escribir un libro como este es que luego lo leerán tus amigos, la gente que te quiere. Y entonces dejarán de quererte. Qué alivio...".

Así comienza esta novela, y esas palabras podrían eximirnos de más comentarios de presentación. También bastaría con reproducir el siguiente diálogo, real, entre un célebre escritor francés y el autor de este libro:

–Tu problema es que escribes pensando en jóvenes rebeldes. Y los que compran libros en esta época no son ni una cosa ni la otra. La rebeldía es un anacronismo. Ya no hay más rebeldes.

–Es cierto. Ni siquiera hay jóvenes.

El mismo sarcástico inconformismo está presente en cada página, montado sobre un humor –en el lenguaje y en las situaciones– que acarrea un efecto residual más bien corrosivo. No es, por cierto, un libro sin contraindicaciones. El delgado hilo conductor del relato es un hecho policial al que ni siquiera el protagonista, a pesar de que podría terminar seriamente comprometido, parece darle demasiada importancia. Porque más que nada la novela es el registro minucioso de la mirada de este protagonista paseándose con una perplejidad disfrazada de cinismo sobre los personajes y las circunstancias de esta época, que él define como "la era del afecto, esa forma bastarda y minusválida de la pasión".

Otros títulos de nuestra editorial